THIS BOOK BELONGS TO:

_____

_____

_____

meomi

WOULD LIKE TO DEDICATE THIS BOOK TO
ALL OUR FRIENDS WHO ALWAYS KNOW
HOW TO CHEER US UP & ON

MEOMI is author/illustrator duo, Vicki Wong and Michael C. Murphy. They live in Vancouver, Canada, where they enjoy writing silly stories, drinking tea and drawing strange creatures. Meomi's art and animation has been featured in numerous books, toys and projects worldwide, notably the Vancouver 2010 Olympic and Paralympic mascots (Quatchi, Miga, Sumi and Mukmuk). Meomi likes blobfish, parlour guitars and bike rides.
Visit them at www.meomi.com.

I HIGHLY RECOMMEND THESE OTHER DELIGHTFUL BOOKS!

First published in hardback in the USA by Immedium Inc. in 2008
First published in hardback and paperback in Great Britain by HarperCollins Children's Books in 2010

10 9 8 7 6

ISBN: 978-0-00-731254-2

HarperCollins Children's Books is a division of HarperCollins Publishers Ltd.

Text and illustrations copyright © MEOMI Design Inc.: Vicki Wong and Michael Murphy 2008

Published by arrangement with Immedium Inc. immedium www.immedium.com
Printed in Hong Kong

Edited by Don Menn and Tracy Swedlow
Design by Meomi and Stefanie Liang

Rainy days are ok.

THE OCTONAUTS

& the Frown Fish

• MEOMI •

HarperCollins *Children's Books*

It was a quiet and rainy afternoon at the bottom of the ocean when...

Professor Inkling was dusting his dust jackets.

Kwazii Kitten was watering his catnip.

Tunip the Vegimal was tossing a salad.

Peso Penguin was pinging...

Tweak Bunny was playing a game.

Captain Barnacles Bear was singing in the rain.

...Shellington Sea Otter was ponging.

Dashi Dog was sounding the Octo-Alert!!!

The crew hurried down to HQ to find Dashi
monitoring the Octopod's screens anxiously.

"There's a fish with a very big frown outside!"
she reported to the others.
"He looks so glum that all the creatures
around him are starting to get upset, too!"

```
**** OCTONET BBS V2 ****
LOAD"FROWN FISH",8,1
 ...SMILEY FISH
 ....ANGRY FISH
 ...HUNGRY FISH
 ...SLEEPY FISH
 ....SILLY FISH
???....FROWN FISH
?FILE NOT FOUND
```

"I can't find a fish like him on the Octonet!"
Dr Shellington said excitedly.
"Could he be a new species?"

"Octonauts, we should investigate!"
Professor Inkling declared.

Up close, the little fish looked even gloomier.
"Why are you so sad?" Dashi asked with concern.
But the fish only replied, "Glub, glub."

GLUB
GLUB
GLUB

What a dilemma! None of the Octonauts spoke Frownese!

On the blackboard:

× GLUB = SOCK
× GLUB = TWO TURNIPS
× GLUB GLUB = COOKIE
GLUB =

KNOW your GERM

"Perhaps if we understood his language, then we could help him," Dr Shellington proposed.

Shellington and Dashi spent hours in the lab trying to learn Frownese, but it proved to be a very difficult language to translate.

"I don't think we can work much longer," Dashi sighed.
"I'm starting to feel unhappy myself! Let's think of other ways to cheer him up."

"Playing music with my friends always brightens my day," Peso shyly suggested.

He invited everyone to pick up an instrument.

As the crew gathered together to play a happy song, other creatures joined in.

There was a clamcapella group, a sea horchestra and a baritone whale!

Unfortunately, the Frown Fish didn't have an ear for music and continued to pout.

"It's hard to feel sad when you're being glamorous!"
Kwazii announced with a flourish.
"Let's have a dressing-up party!"

The little fish tried on many different costumes...

COWBOY

GHOST

PRINCESS

MAGIC USER LVL 20

VAMPIRE

BUMBLEBEE

CLOWN

DOCTOR

ICE CREAM

ROCK STAR

FRANKENSTEIN

...but none of them could disguise his sadness.

Dashi held up her favourite camera and asked,
"Why don't we visit the famous Snail Gardens?
We could have a photography field trip!"

The Octonauts took photos of big snails and little snails, striped snails and polka dot snails. The Frown Fish, however, wouldn't even smile for the camera.

SNAIL RAIL

"A game of miniature golf always tickles my fancy!" revealed Dr Shellington.
The group putted and swung their way through many aquatic obstacles:
sandshark traps, sea dragons and electric eel tunnels.

The Frown Fish scored a hole-in-one on the King Crab course but he didn't look any happier.

"I like working with my paws. Let's build something!"
Tweak suggested. Surrounded by gadgets and contraptions,
the crew constructed a robo-tank for the Frown Fish.

Tweak stood back and admired their work. "Now our friend can use his new sea legs to visit us inside the Octopod!"

If possible, the Frown Fish looked even frownier!

Tunip chirped eagerly as it led the group into the kitchen.
"Vegimals love to cook and bake. Maybe the Frown Fish is hungry?"
Dr Shellington interpreted helpfully.

The whole crew set out to make their favourite pastries.
They baked barnacle cakes, barnacle muffins and even a fancy barnacle soufflé.

The Frown Fish ate an entire plate of biscuits, but he still looked unsatisfied.

"There's nothing like perusing the printed word to stimulate the intellect and galvanise the imagination!" Professor Inkling exclaimed to a confused crew.

"To the library, my delightful colleagues!"

Professor Inkling read from his favourite book of jokes,
but the Frown Fish didn't laugh once.
"Frown Fish must not have funny bones," Inkling decided.
The other Octonauts weren't too sure...
they didn't get the jokes either.

"I always feel better after I exercise!" Captain Barnacles said.
The Octonauts swooshed down the slide,
clambered up the climbing frame and rode the see-saw.

Peso and the Frown Fish sat on the merry-go-round
while Kwazii pushed them faster and faster until...

WHOOOP!

WHOOOP! The Frown Fish flew right off!

The little fish

TURNED...

BOUNCED...

AND ROLLED OVER.

Everyone rushed over in alarm.
They had only been trying to cheer him up,
but now he might be hurt!

To the Octonauts' surprise, the Frown Fish had a BIG smile on his face!

"Of course!" Professor Inkling realised.
   "He's not a frown fish... he's an upside-down fish!"

ENCYCLOPEDIA AQUATICA

UPSIDE-DOWN CATFISH
(Synodontis nigriventris)

These whiskered fish like to spend time upside down. They also enjoy music, costume parties, field trips, miniature golf, tinkering, baking, reading and exercising.

263

(Synodontis nigriventris)

"There are different types of fish that swim upside down; it's easier for them to spot food.
   This chap is a fine example of an Upside-Down Catfish!"

Everyone laughed in relief to discover that
their new friend had been smiling the whole day!
The catfish made a big "ERP!" and turned himself
back upside-down... or was it right side up?

MEET THE OCTONAUTS!

CAPTAIN BARNACLES

Brave Captain Barnacles is a polar bear extraordinaire and leader of the Octonauts crew. He is always the first to rush in and help when there is trouble. Besides adventuring, Barnacles enjoys playing his accordion and writing in his captain's log.

LIEUTENANT KWAZII

Kwazii is a daredevil orange kitten from the mysterious Far East. This cat loves excitement and travelling to exotic places. Favourite pastimes include long baths, sword fighting and general swashbuckling.

NURSE PESO

Peso is the medic for the team. He enjoys putting bandages on cuts and tending to wounds. He's not too fond of scary things, but fortunately his big heart usually wins over monsters.

DR SHELLINGTON

Shellington is a nerdy sea otter scientist who loves doing field research and lab work. He is easily distracted by rare plants and animals, which means he sometimes needs the other Octonauts to help him out of sticky situations.

TWEAK BUNNY

Tweak is the engineer for the Octopod. She keeps everything working properly below deck in the engine room and maintains the Octonauts' subs, GUP-A to GUP-E. Tweak loves all kinds of machinery and enjoys tinkering with strange contraptions that sometimes work in unexpected ways.

DASHI DOG

Dashi is the sweet dachshund dog who oversees operations in the Octopod control room and launch bay. She manages all ship traffic and ensures all the computers are in good working order. She also loves photographing all the wonderful underwater plants and animals.

PROFESSOR INKLING

Professor Inkling is a brilliant Dumbo octopus oceanographer. He founded the Octonauts with the intention of furthering underwater research and preservation. Because of his size and delicate, big brain, he prefers to help out the team from the safety of the Octopod.

TUNIP THE VEGIMAL

Discovered by Dr Shellington, Tunip is one of many Vegimals, a special breed of underwater critter (part animal / part vegetable) who like to help out around the Octopod. Vegimals love to cook barnacle dishes: barnacle pasta, barnacle cakes, barnacle cookies...